If You Were a Dog

For Jon, a best-friend-ever sort of husband.
Thank you to Janine O'Malley, FSG, and the Hamline
University M.F.A. program faculty and staff. —J.S.

For Keith —C.R.

Farrar Straus Giroux Books for Young Readers
175 Fifth Avenue, New York 10010

Text copyright © 2014 by Jamie Swenson
Pictures copyright © 2014 by Chris Raschka
All rights reserved
Color separations by Bright Arts (H.K.) Ltd.
Printed in China by South China Printing Co. Ltd.,
Dongguan City, Guangdong Province
First edition, 2014
1 3 5 7 9 10 8 6 4 2

mackids.com

Library of Congress Cataloging-in-Publication Data
Swenson, Jamie.
    If you were a dog / Jamie Swenson ; pictures by Chris Raschka. — 1st ed.
        p.   cm.
    Summary: Easy-to-read text invites the reader to imagine life as a dog, a cat,
a fish, a bird, and even a dinosaur.
    ISBN 978-0-374-33530-4
    [1. Animals—Fiction.   2. Imagination—Fiction.]   I. Raschka, Christopher, ill.   II. TItle.

PZ7.S9748835If 2013
[E]—dc23   2011034922

Farrar Straus Giroux Books for Young Readers may be purchased for business
or promotional use. For information on bulk purchases please contact
Macmillan Corporate and Premium Sales Department at
(800) 221-7945 x5442 or by email at specialmarkets@macmillan.com.

If You Were a Dog

Jamie A. Swenson

Pictures by **Chris Raschka**

Farrar Straus Giroux / New York

If you were a dog, would you be a speedy-quick,

lickety-sloppidy,

scavenge-the-garbage,

frisbee-catching,

hot-dog-stealing,

pillow-hogging,

best-friend-ever sort of dog?

Would you howl at the moon?

ARRRRRR

OOOOOOOOOOOO!

Some dogs do.

If you were a cat,
would you be a

purr-purr-purr-purring,
furry-stretching,

tuna-fish-eating,

sandpaper-licking,

bird-stalking,

yarn-tangling,

soft-as-a-whisper,
creeping—POUNCING—sort of cat?

Would you hiss at dogs?

SSSSSSSSSSSSSSSSSSS SS!

Some cats do.

If you were a fish, would you be a

sea-sparkler, ocean-swimming,

coral-peeker,

wave-jumping,

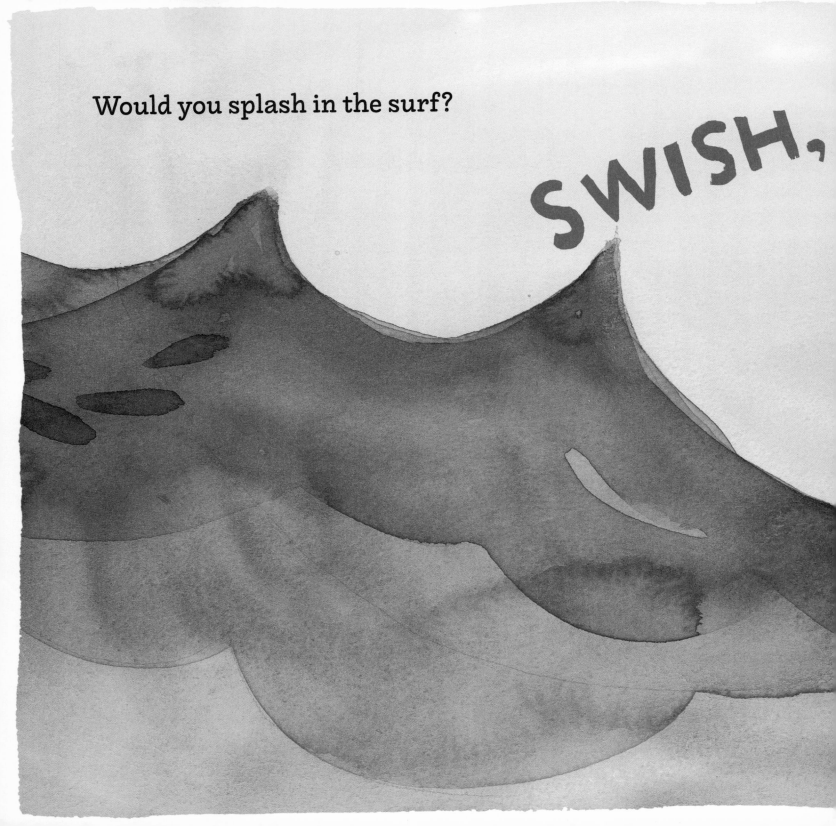

SWISH, SWISH!

Some fish do.

If you were a bird,
would you be a

trout-snatching,

swooping,
soaring,
sky-circling,

screeching-tweeter,

berry-eater,

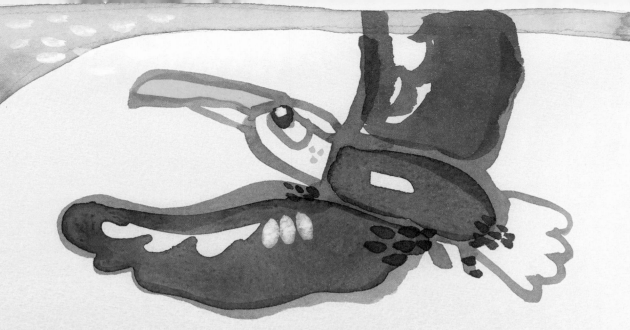

mountain-gliding,

dino-eyed,
perching-raptor
sort of bird?

Would you wing to the clouds?

OOSH, SWOOSH, SWOOSH!

Some birds do.

If you were a bug,
would you be a

flutter-by-er,
zooming-higher,

inching-creeper,

flower-keeper,

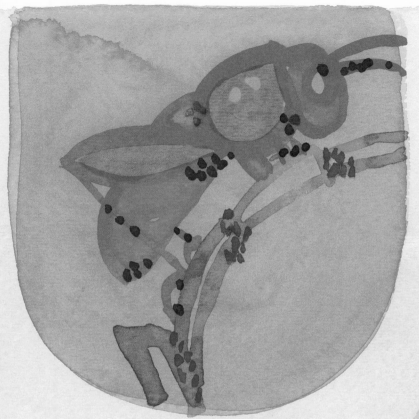

never-stinging,
buzzing-chirper,

water-gliding-skimmer
sort of bug?

Would you sing the whole night through?

CRIK, CRIK, CRIK!

Some bugs do.

If you were a frog,
would you be a

giant-hopper,
ribbety-racer,

mighty-jumper,

dragonfly-chaser,

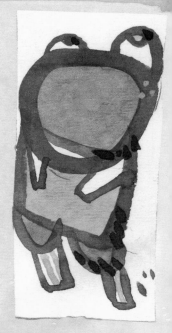

lily-pad-bumper,

croaking-ballooner,

summer-night-crooner
sort of frog?

Would you spring and zing
and hop all day?

BOING,

BOING, RIBBET!

Some frogs do.

If you were a dinosaur,
would you be a stomping-roarer,
earth-quaker, tree-shaker,

sharp-pointed
toothy-grinner,

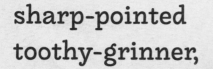

colossal-chomper,

super-duper, longest-neck-o-saur
sort of dinosaur?

Would you eat trees?

CHOMP, STOMP,

ROAR!

Some dinosaurs did.

But you are not

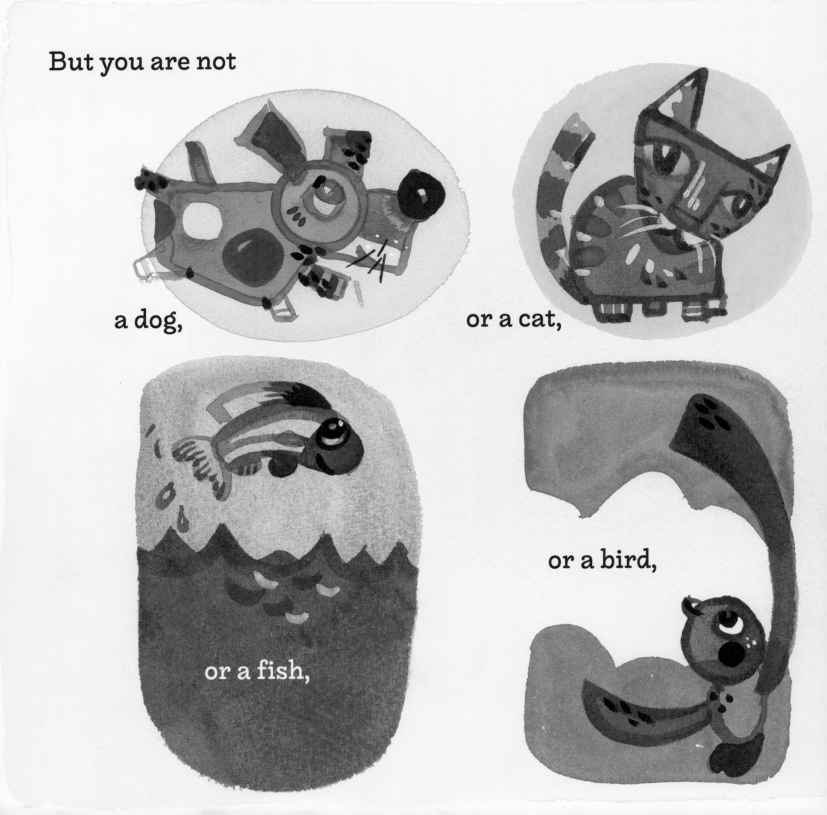

a dog,

or a cat,

or a fish,

or a bird,

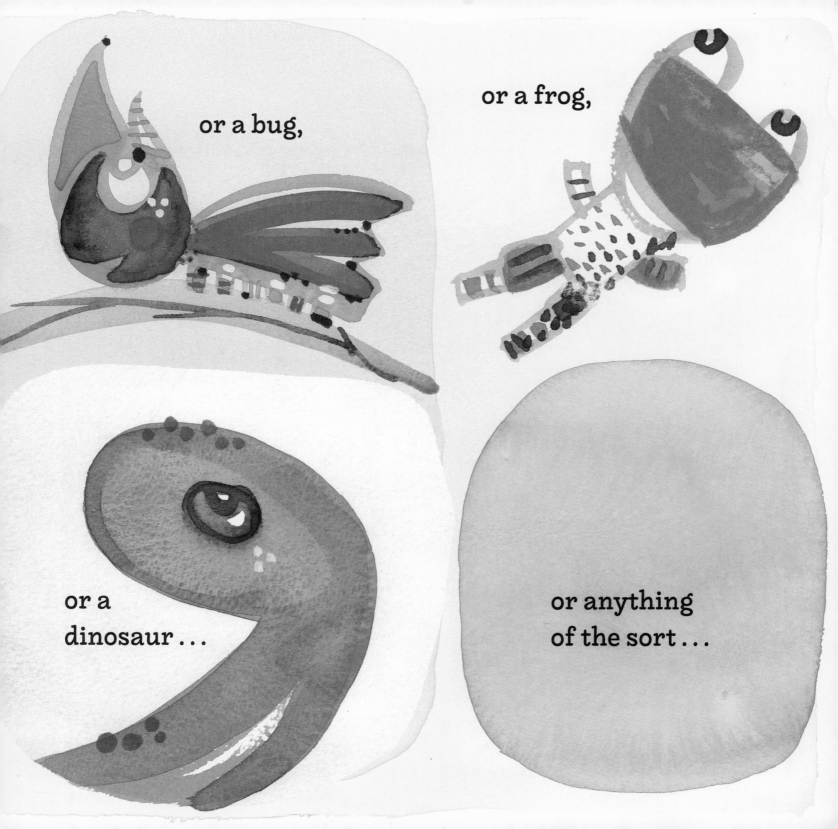

or a bug,

or a frog,

or a dinosaur . . .

or anything of the sort . . .

You can

ARRROOOOOOOo!

HISSSSSS!

like a dog,

like a cat,

SWISH, SWISH, SWISH!

like a fish,

BOING, BOING, RIBBET!

like a frog,

SWOOSH, SWOOSH, SWOOSH!

like a bird,

CHOMP, STOMP, ROAR!

like a dinosaur, and . . .

CRIK, CRIK, CRIK!

like a bug,

GIGGLE,

GIGGLE, GIGGLE!

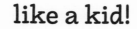

like a kid!

And that is the very best

sort of thing to be.